The

Magical Friends Forever

Special thanks to Sue Mongredien

First published in 2010
by Faber and Faber Ltd
Bloomsbury House
74–77 Great Russell Street
London WC1B 3DA

Printed in England by Bookmarque, Croydon, UK

Series created by Working Partners Limited, London W6 0QT

A CIP record for this book
is available from the British Library

978–0–571–24805–6

2 4 6 8 10 9 7 5 3 1

The HOOZLES™
Magical Friends Forever

A Penguin Problem

By Jessie Little

Illustrated by Penny Dann

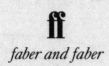

faber and faber

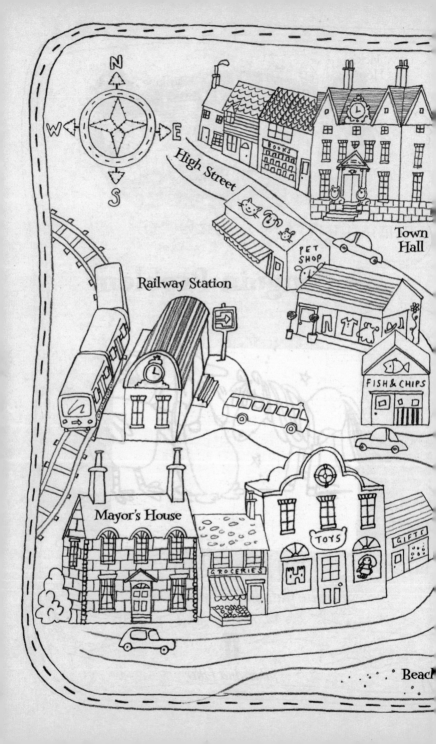

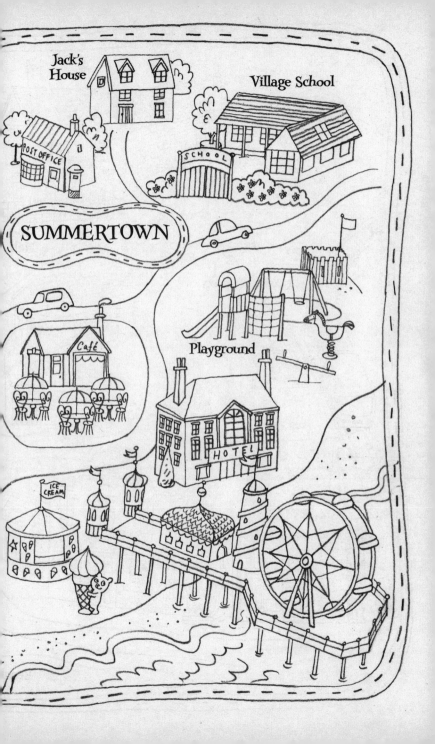

Chapter One

'This is going to look so cool!' Willow
Thompson said with a grin, as she
arranged a group of dolls around a
miniature wooden table. She was kneeling
in the window of her Auntie Suzy's toy

shop helping her aunt and brother, Freddie, set up a new doll's house display there. The shop was closed and the blind had been pulled down so that nobody could see in from outside.

'Glad you think so,' Auntie Suzy replied, her eyes twinkling. 'I've got some tiny dolls' food here, Willow. Why don't you put some on the table for them?'

Willow took the miniature plates and buns her aunt was passing her and set them out in front of the dolls. There was a tiny blue teapot which she put in the middle, and matching cups and saucers. There! The sweetest tea party you could imagine.

It was Sunday evening, and Willow knew that in all the shops nearby the shopkeepers would be hard at work creating their own imaginative displays. This was because every summer, for five days known as 'Wacky Windows Week', the shops along the Summertown seafront each prepared special window displays, one for every day from Monday to Friday. Willow was looking forward to seeing the other shop windows but she knew already that theirs would be hard to beat.

Freddie, who was five, was carefully putting the smallest doll in a little pink crib, up in one of the top rooms. 'Night night,' he said, tucking a dainty pink blanket over her.

'Talking of "night night",' Auntie Suzy said, 'I think it's about time you got in your PJs, Freddie. Come on.' She lifted him out of the display and took him upstairs to brush his teeth.

Willow was seven, and went to bed half an hour later than Freddie, so she began arranging some dolls in the living room, the last room that needed setting up. She put one doll on the sofa watching the miniature TV set. She sat another doll in a red armchair, reading a tiny book.

'You could have one of them talking on the phone,' suggested a low rumbly sort of voice from nearby.

Willow jumped at the sound, and knocked over the tiny television. She'd been concentrating so hard, she'd almost forgotten Toby was there beside her. Toby was Willow's Hoozle, a lovely cuddly blue bear with velvety bits on his paws. He'd always been Willow's favourite toy – Auntie Suzy had made him for her. But it was only when she and Freddie had come to stay with Auntie Suzy for the summer that Willow had discovered just how special Toby was – he could talk and move, and was just as much alive as her!

'Good thinking,' Willow said to him, giving him a little squeeze before standing one of the dolls in the corner with the tiny white phone pressed into her hand. 'There,' she said, gazing proudly at the whole scene. 'Finished – and doesn't it look wonderful?'

Toby wriggled happily in her arms as they both looked at the display. As well as the house full of busy dolls, there was also a beautiful piece of green velvet for a garden, complete with miniature plastic trees, and dolls leaning back in little deckchairs or playing hide and seek.

Toby gave a throaty growl of pleasure. 'Perfect,' he said. 'Just perfect!'

Unfortunately, the next morning when Willow and Auntie Suzy came down to the shop, the display looked anything but perfect. Someone – or something – had knocked over half the dolls, and the furniture was all higgledy-piggledy.

'How did this happen?' Willow cried in dismay, kneeling down and trying to fix the spoiled garden.

'I wonder if a cat got in?' Auntie Suzy said thoughtfully. 'Ahh – the back window

is open a crack, look. Maybe an animal squeezed in there. How annoying!' She sighed. 'Ah well. Come on, let's sort it out quickly before we open up.'

Willow glanced at Toby as she and her aunt began fixing the display. She wasn't so sure it was a cat who'd knocked over the display. In Willow's mind, there was a far more likely culprit – Croc, the bad-tempered crocodile Hoozle, who seemed to delight in causing trouble. Toby gave a tiny nod, as if reading Willow's mind. Croc didn't live at Auntie Suzy's shop and it was just the sort of mean thing he would think of!

'At last,' Auntie Suzy said, once they'd re-done the display. 'That will have to do.'

'It's not as good as it was last night

though,' Willow said, feeling disappointed.

'No, we've run out of time, I'm afraid,' Auntie Suzy told her. 'I need to open up. Never mind. We'll make tomorrow's display extra special instead.' And with that, she pulled up the blinds, and turned the shop sign to 'Open'.

A small crowd had gathered outside the toy shop and Auntie Suzy went to talk to them. Willow seized the chance to go over to the Hoozle Council, a group of three other Hoozles who lived in the shop. 'Hi, guys,' she said in a low voice. 'Did you see anything suspicious last night?'

'Aaatchoozle!' spluttered Grouchy, the fat penguin Hoozle, his beak trembling as he sneezed. 'Oh, this cold! It's driving me nuts!'

Wizard, who was an owl-shaped Hoozle, and the leader of the Hoozle Council, put a kindly wing around Grouchy. 'Did we see anything suspicious? No,' he replied, peering down at Willow. 'I slept very deeply. Didn't hear a thing.'

'Nor me,' said Lovely, tossing her mane out of her eyes. She was a horse Hoozle who'd once belonged to Willow's mum. She grinned mischievously. 'Maybe it was the force of Grouchy's sneezes that blew over the display.'

Willow smiled. 'Poor Grouchy, it's horrid having a cold in the summer.' But before

she could say any more, Auntie Suzy
was back in the shop, with a group of
customers. She wandered away, thinking
hard. If Croc had messed up the display,
why had he done such a horrible thing?
And would he be back again that night?

Chapter Two

That afternoon, Auntie Suzy left her
assistant Ricky in charge of the shop and
took Willow and Freddie along the seafront
to look at the other windows. It was such
fun – they all looked so different. Willow's
favourite was the cake shop which had a
huge cake in the middle, made to look just
like a teddy bear. She held Toby up to the
window to show him. 'Look, it's nearly as
cute as you,' she said, dropping a kiss on his
head.

Once they'd had tea and the toy shop
was closed, it was time to begin the next
window display. This time, they set up
an elaborate model railway, with lots of
bridges, points and passengers to pick up
from the stations. Freddie loved trains, so
he particularly enjoyed arranging it. 'This
is just like playing,' he said happily, as he
clipped pieces of tunnel together.

'Ready for the grand switch-on?' Auntie
Suzy asked when they'd finished. 'Three,
two, one . . . go!' She pressed a button, and

the small electric engines whirred into life, trundling along the tracks with their carriages bumping behind them.

'Yay!' cheered Willow and Freddie.

'It looks brilliant,' Willow added, smiling up at her aunt.

'Thanks to you two,' Auntie Suzy replied. 'And I'll make sure all the windows are shut tight tonight. We don't want any stray moggies clambering in again, do we?'

'No way,' said Freddie.

Willow glanced up at the Hoozle Council on their high shelf and gave them a meaningful look. We don't want naughty Croc spoiling our display, you mean! she thought to herself.

The next morning, Willow woke up early and the first thing that popped into her head was the model railway. 'Come on,' she said to Toby, pulling on her dressing gown. 'Let's go and make sure it's all right.'

With Toby in her arms, she padded downstairs and into the shop. 'Oh no!' she groaned as soon as she saw the display. The model railway had been ruined, with parts of the track scattered all over the place and one of the engines missing.

The Hoozles woke at her cry, blinking and stretching on their shelf. Grouchy gave a huge aaahchoozle! and rubbed his pink-rimmed eyes.

'Oh dear,' Lovely said, trotting from shelf to shelf until she reached Willow. 'I can't believe it's happened again. And I slept right through the whole thing!'

Wizard peered down at the mess. 'Who could have done this? I know Suzy locked up very carefully last night – I watched her to make sure.'

He and Grouchy made their way down to Willow and they all worked quickly to put the model railway back as it had been. Grouchy found the missing engine behind one of the shelves and Wizard pecked the pieces of track back into place.

'I'm sure it's Croc,' Willow fumed. 'But how is he getting in? And why is he so determined to wreck our lovely window displays?'

Lovely sighed. 'He's a nasty piece of work,' she said, wrinkling her nose. 'He should be ashamed of himself – but he probably isn't.'

'Well, if he tries it again tonight, I'm going to stop him,' Willow vowed. 'I'll stay up all night if I have to, and I'll catch him in the act!'

That afternoon, Willow and Freddie went out with Auntie Suzy again to see the other shop windows. 'Oh, look at the grocer's display!' Willow called in delight, as she noticed that all the fruit and vegetables had been arranged in the shape of flowers. 'Isn't it pretty?'

Auntie Suzy chuckled. 'I love that one,' she said, pointing to a flower that had a cabbage middle and courgettes as petals. 'Oh, and look how all those grapes have been arranged in the shape of leaves! Almost too good to eat!'

'Hi, Willow. Hi, Freddie. Hi, Suzy,' came a voice just then.

Willow turned away from the window to see Jack, a boy who'd come to the shop just the week before to buy an elephant Hoozle, Bouncer.

'Hi, Jack!' Willow said, smiling and making Toby's arm wave to Bouncer. 'How are you?'

Jack made Bouncer wave back to Toby.

'We're good,' Jack said, and started talking about the special den he'd made for Bouncer in his bedroom.

Willow couldn't concentrate though, because Toby was pressing the side of her arm. Why was he doing that? she wondered in surprise. If anyone saw him moving, their secret would be out!

Then she realised what Toby had just seen and gasped. A fluffy orange tail was disappearing into the alley down the side of the grocer's shop. Croc!

Chapter Three

Willow thought fast. 'Um . . . I'll see you soon, Jack,' she blurted out. 'I just remembered I need to be someplace else . . .' And she darted into the alley without another word, her heart thumping. She felt a bit rude, rushing away from Jack so abruptly, but this was important. Where was Croc?

Unfortunately the orange crocodile Hoozle had vanished from sight. Willow looked around a couple of wooden crates and peered under some cardboard boxes, but there was no sign of him.

'He's crafty,' Toby said crossly. 'Probably watching us from a hiding place somewhere.'

Willow glanced over her shoulder. She could hear Auntie Suzy calling her. 'Well, if you dare come into the shop tonight, Croc, I'll be waiting for you,' she said in a low voice. 'I won't let you get away with it again!'

That evening, Willow helped her aunt and brother set up the next window display. This time it was a medieval scene, with a princess, a knight, and a big red dragon outside a castle. Auntie Suzy had even managed to rig up a moat with water flowing around the castle!

'This is my favourite one,' Freddie said, beaming as he fixed a tiny silver sword into the knight's hand. 'Even better than the trains.'

'It's brilliant,' Willow agreed. And I'll make sure it still looks as good by tomorrow! she thought to herself. That mean Croc will be sorry if I catch him!

That night, she forced herself to stay

awake until she'd heard Auntie Suzy go to bed, then she got up with Toby and hid on the stairs. She planned to stay there the whole night, listening out for anyone breaking into the shop. 'I'm definitely going to catch the window-wrecker tonight,' Willow said to Toby, smothering a little yawn.

'Absolutely,' Toby replied, from where he was cuddled up in her lap. 'We'll put a stop to them, won't we, Willow? Willow?'

Willow had curled into a more comfortable position, and was resting her head on her arms. 'I'm just shutting my eyes for a minute,' she said

drowsily. 'I'll still be listening out though, don't worry . . .'

'Willow! Willow! Wake up!'

'What's happening? Who's that?' Willow blinked blearily, still half-asleep as Toby shook her with his soft paws. Then she sat up and stared around. She was back in her bed, under the duvet . . . and sunlight was pouring through the window. 'How did I get in here?' she asked, confused. Just a minute ago, she'd been on the stairs with Toby, listening out for the intruder.

Toby gave a sigh. 'Willow, you dozed off on the stairs. I heard a voice and tried to wake you up but you were just so fast asleep, I couldn't do it. Your aunt found you on the stairs a bit later and carried you back to bed.'

Willow rubbed her eyes, trying to take all of this in. 'You heard a voice?' she asked him. 'A voice in the shop?'

'Two voices,' Toby said, 'but they were very whispery. I heard one of them say, "They will never suspect you", but everything else was too quiet for me to make out. I tried to open the shop door but it was so heavy I couldn't do it.' His furry shoulders drooped. 'Sorry, Willow. I let you down.'

Willow hugged him tightly. 'You didn't,' she told him. 'It was my stupid fault, falling asleep like that. Come on,' she said, swinging her legs out of bed. 'Let's go downstairs now and see what's happened to the window. Maybe it was the Hoozles you heard talking in the night, and the display will be fine.'

She hurried down to the shop with Toby and saw to her disappointment that, once more, the window display had been ruined. The castle had been knocked over, with the characters and dragon scattered across the floor. 'Oh no!' Willow groaned. 'Not again!'

Wizard hopped down from his shelf, followed by Lovely and Grouchy. 'We'll help,' Wizard offered. 'It's the least we can do for sleeping through the break-in for the third night on the trot.' He frowned. 'I can't understand how we haven't been woken up by the noise. Whoever is getting in here manages to do it very quietly.'

Willow heard footsteps overhead, and set to work rebuilding the castle wall as quickly as she could manage. 'We'll have to hurry,' she said. 'I think that was Auntie Suzy I just heard upstairs. She'll be down to open the shop soon, and we can't let her see this mess.'

'Here's the princess's tiara – but it's bent out of shape,' Lovely said sadly, pulling it out from under the table.

'Here's the knight's helmet,' Wizard said, his sharp eyes spotting it in a corner.

Willow flew around, trying to remember where everything had been the night before. She had just stuck the last flag back on the castle tower when she heard Auntie Suzy and Freddie coming downstairs. 'Quick, back to your shelf!' she hissed to Lovely and Wizard, who hurried away at once. 'Where's Grouchy?'

'He's down here,' Toby said, pulling at the little penguin, who'd fallen asleep under the display table. 'Grouchy! Wake up. Suzy alert!'

Grouchy blinked and shook out his wings. 'Sorry,' he murmured, waddling quickly away towards the Hoozle shelf. 'So tired. Just so tired.'

'Phew,' Willow sighed, picking up Toby

and giving him a hug. 'That's better.'

Auntie Suzy came in at that moment and raised her eyebrows at the sight of Willow, still in her pyjamas, standing in the shop. 'Everything all right?' she asked.

Willow blushed, hoping her aunt wouldn't ask why she'd been sleeping on the stairs the night before. 'Fine,' she said, avoiding her aunt's gaze. 'Just going to have some breakfast.'

She ducked out of the shop before Auntie Suzy could say anything else and went upstairs. As she did so, she remembered what Toby had said he'd heard. Two voices . . . could it mean that Croc had found somebody to help with his naughty plans? If so . . . who was it?

Chapter Four

'Oh, cool – look, it's Rapunzel and Peter
Pan!' Willow said, as she peered into the
book-shop window on the high street.
She, Freddie and Auntie Suzy had come
out to see the other
shop displays that
morning, and this was
her favourite so far. The
shop owner's eldest
two children, Beth and
Leo, were in there dressed

up as story-book characters and waving at passers-by.

'Lovely,' Auntie Suzy said, waving back at them. 'Oh, and that must be Sleeping Beauty, bless her,' she said, pointing at their younger sister Lily, who was only two, curled up fast asleep on a big cushion.

'Don't they look great?' a friendly woman said, who had a little girl with her. 'And we're looking forward to seeing your toy shop window on Friday, Suzy – we always love to see the Hoozles in their very own display!'

'Oh yes,' said the girl eagerly. 'I love that cute penguin Hoozle – he's so adorable, isn't he?'

Willow smiled. 'He's really sweet,' she agreed, thinking that she should remember to tell Grouchy that later on. He needed something to cheer him up, after suffering with his cold all week.

That night, Willow, Suzy and Freddie set to work on Thursday's shop window – a whole town made of interlocking building blocks. Willow had been thinking all day about how she could catch the window-wrecker and had come up with a plan. She would set a booby-trap so that if anyone tried to spoil the display, they'd get caught. Now . . . what would a window-wrecker be sure to go for in this particular arrangement?

She grinned as her eye fell on a large clock tower that Freddie was building right in the middle of the window. Of course. A big tower was the obvious target. Now she just had to set up a little surprise for anyone who tried to knock it over . . .

As soon as her aunt took Freddie off to bed, Willow set to work. She nipped behind the shop counter and found the ball of string, which her aunt sometimes used for wrapping parcels. She hid the string at the base of the tall clock tower and stared thoughtfully above it. As luck would have it, there was a hook in the ceiling directly above the tower, where her aunt often hung puppets or costumes. 'Perfect,' she said under her breath.

'What are you plotting?' Toby asked curiously, seeing her gazing up at it.

'I'm plotting to catch a croc,' Willow said with a grin. 'He's in for a shock tonight all right!'

Willow was tired that evening but forced
herself to stay awake until Auntie Suzy
had gone to bed. Then she got up with
Toby and crept into the utility room where
the cleaning things were kept. There was
just enough moonlight shining through
the window for Willow to see the big red
bucket that was stowed with the
mop in the corner.

Toby rubbed his eyes with
his paws. 'What do you
need that
for?' he
whispered
as Willow
carried
him and
the bucket

downstairs to the shop.

Willow explained her plan in a low voice. 'We're going to tie one end of the string to the bucket handle and hang it upside-down from the ceiling hook above the tower of blocks,' she hissed. 'Then I'll wedge the rest of the string tightly inside the tower. As soon as the tower gets knocked over, the string will be released . . . and the bucket will fall down on Croc!'

Toby held up his paw for a high-five.

'Genius,' he said, with a low rumbly laugh. 'Utter genius.'

Willow high-fived him with a grin. 'Come on,' she said, 'let's set up the trap. We'll have to be quiet though, so we don't wake the other Hoozles.'

She gently pushed the shop door open then tiptoed through. It was dark in there, but she could just make out the shadowy figures of the sleeping Hoozles up on the shelf. Taking great care not to make a sound, Willow crept over to the building-block tower and lifted out the ball of string. Then she pulled out about two metres of it, and handed the end to Toby, who scrambled up the nearest shelf and, leaning out daringly, managed to throw it over the ceiling hook.

Willow gave him the thumbs-up sign then quickly tied the end of the string to the bucket handle. She pulled the string so that the bucket was hoisted up into the air, then, by standing on a chair and keeping

the string taut, managed to tip the bucket over so that it sat upside-down against the ceiling.

Phew! Now she needed to wedge the ball of string back into the tower, and the trap was set. Very very carefully, hardly daring to breathe for fear of knocking over the bricks, she slid the ball of string inside the tower's base and weighted it there with a heavy rectangular brick.

She took her hand away, half-expecting the string to loosen and the bucket to fall but . . . nothing happened. The trap was set!

'Nicely done,' Toby whispered approvingly. Willow nodded, carrying him back out of the shop and sitting down with him on the stairs outside.

'Now all we have to do,' she said, 'is wait.'

Chapter Five

This time, Willow was determined not to
fall asleep. She and Toby played whispered
games of I-Spy to keep them from dozing
off, but all remained quiet in the shop for
a long while . . . until, at last, they heard a
loud crash – and then a surprised yelp.

Willow felt instantly wide awake and
jumped to her feet, grabbing Toby and
rushing through to the shop. 'What's going
on?' she heard Wizard exclaim but she only
had eyes for the bucket, which was now

twitching in
the middle of
the display.

Willow ran
over and lifted
the bucket.
'Gotcha!'
she cried
triumphantly.

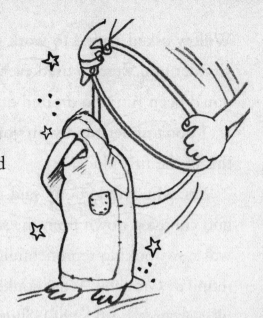

Then she
stared. 'Grouchy?' she said, baffled, staring
at the little penguin who had been trapped
underneath the bucket. 'What are you
doing there?'

'Was it you all along?' Toby cried in
disbelief. 'We thought it was Croc!'

Grouchy stared at his webbed feet. 'It was
me and Croc,' he confessed.

'So you were letting him in, were you?'

Willow asked, trying to work it out. 'No wonder you were so tired every day if you'd been running around at night. But . . . I don't understand why you would do this in the first place?'

'Yes, why would you?' said Lovely, who had cantered down from the shelves and was now looking reproachfully through her mane at Grouchy. 'How could you? We've all seen how hard Suzy, Willow and Freddie have worked every evening, putting the beautiful displays together.'

Grouchy hung his head. 'I hate Wacky Windows Week,' he said miserably. 'I always get stuck in the middle of the Hoozle display, and I hate being stared at.' A tear plopped from his eye. 'Nobody's ever wanted me for their toy and it just makes me feel worse, all those children looking at me but none of them wanting to buy me. And Croc said . . . Croc said . . .'

'What did Croc say?' Willow asked gently.

Grouchy's velvety shoulders were shaking. 'He said that nobody would ever love me,' he got out. 'And he said that if I messed up Wacky Windows Week, I wouldn't have to sit in the window and be stared at.' A tear rolled down his beak. 'I'm sorry. I know I shouldn't have done it but . . .'

Willow hugged Grouchy close.

'Everybody loves you!' she told him. 'All the Hoozles, me and Freddie, and Auntie Suzy!'

'Just because you don't have a child doesn't mean you're not loved,' Wizard put in.

'Not at all!' Lovely agreed.

Grouchy tried to smile but Willow could tell he still didn't feel happy. She quickly put the tower back up, wished the Hoozles all good night, then went back to bed. She had to think of a way to convince poor Grouchy that he was loved – but how?

★ ★ ★

'Hi Willow – oh, is that the penguin Hoozle you've got there?' the lady from the bakery asked with a smile the next day. 'He is so cute, isn't he?'

Willow smiled back. 'He's a sweetheart,' she agreed. Over breakfast, she'd remembered the girl's comment from the day before about Grouchy being adorable, and she'd decided to take Grouchy out and about, in the hope that he'd realise just how popular he was. So far her plan was working wonderfully – people kept commenting on the little penguin, and telling Willow that he was their favourite Hoozle in Suzy's toy shop.

'There,' Willow said to Grouchy as they reached the seafront, having stopped for another two people to fuss over him along the way. 'Don't you see? Everyone loves you, Grouchy!'

Grouchy looked rather embarrassed but pleased, too. 'Thank you, Willow,' he said gruffly. 'I don't feel so sad about not belonging to a child any more. Now I know I belong to the whole town.' He smiled. 'And I belong with the Hoozles. I see that now.'

'Good for you,' Toby said from where he was tucked into Willow's backpack.

'It's great to see you happy again,' Willow said. 'In fact,' she went on, realising that they were right outside a café, 'I think this calls for an ice cream. Come on!'

Inside the café, Willow struggled to get her money out of her purse with Grouchy still in her arms so she popped him down on a nearby table while she asked for a

chocolate cone. She'd only turned away for
a few minutes but when she turned back
to get Grouchy, she was shocked to see the
table empty. He'd gone!

Chapter Six

'Down there,' Toby hissed from the
backpack. 'I can see an orange tail under
the table.'

Willow looked down. The fluffy orange
tail belonged to Croc . . . and there was
Grouchy under the table with him. What
was going on now?

'You've done a great job messing up
those windows,' Croc was saying, patting
Grouchy on the back. 'Shame that stupid
girl keeps fixing them again. We make a

good team, you and me. And you know, if you wanted to join me, you'd be free from Wacky Windows Week for the rest of your life.'

Willow held her breath, hoping that Grouchy wouldn't want anything to do with naughty Croc again. Thankfully Grouchy was shaking his head. 'I want to stay where I am,' he said stoutly. 'I know now that lots of people do like me. I feel really bad about spoiling the window displays, and I'm not going to let any more be wrecked.'

Croc gave a sneer. 'Ha! The Hoozles window will be ruined, and you can't stop me!' he said. And before Willow could grab hold of him, he'd run off.

Willow picked up Grouchy and cuddled him. 'I heard all of that,' she told him, 'and I'm really glad you chose to stay with the Hoozles. But what will Croc do to the window this time, do you think?'

Grouchy was quivering. 'I don't know,' he said. 'Something horrible, I'm sure.'

'Let's go back to the shop,' Willow decided. 'If Croc's in the mood to cause trouble, anything could happen.'

She hurried back up from the seafront, just in time to see her aunt pulling down the shop blinds and flipping the sign on the door to 'closed'. 'Just popping to the grocer's with Freddie,' Auntie Suzy said. 'I'll be back soon.'

'OK,' said Willow. Then, as the door shut behind them, Grouchy jumped out of Willow's hands and made his way back up to the other Hoozles. 'I'm sorry,' he said to them. 'I've realised today just how lucky I am to have you two. I'm glad you're my friends.'

'Oh, we're glad too!' Lovely whinnied, nuzzling against Grouchy.

Wizard hugged him. 'Good to have you

back,' he said kindly.

Just then, Willow heard a
squeaky sound, coming from
outside. She opened the shop
door and peered around it
to see Croc there, with a
piece of soap on the end of
a stick, covering the window
in thick white streaks. So

that was his plan – he was hoping that by soaping the window, nobody would be able to see the display on the other side of it.

'Hey!' Willow shouted, grabbing Croc and taking him back inside the shop. 'You've got some explaining to do, Mister Croc.'

'Yes, Croc,' Wizard said, looking down his beak at the cross little crocodile who was wriggling furiously in Willow's arms. 'Why on earth have you been trying to spoil Suzy's window displays?'

Croc looked sullen. 'I wanted everyone to think her windows looked rubbish,' he muttered. 'I didn't want anyone to enjoy stupid Wacky Windows Week!'

'Well, everyone loves Wacky Windows Week,' Willow told him. 'So you might as well stop trying to wreck the displays because your stupid plan won't work. Oh, and you can jolly well clean the soap off this window too.'

Croc blew a raspberry at her and tried to leap out of her arms, but Willow held tightly on to him. 'Oh no, you don't!' she said, taking him up to the utility room. 'I've not finished with you yet.'

She filled a bucket of water and got a sponge, then watched over Croc as he grumpily cleaned the soap marks from the window. Once he'd washed them all off, the glass looked wonderfully sparkly. 'People will be able to see the window display even better now it's so spotless,' Willow told him with a wink as she finally let him go. He slouched away, looking defeated, and Willow felt quite sure that he wouldn't be back to bother them for a while.

'Goodness,' Auntie Suzy said, coming

back at that moment, 'doesn't that look clean? Well done, Willow. Our last display of the week will look even more special now!'

Willow grinned. 'With the Hoozles starring in the display, I think it's going to be the best one yet,' she said, stroking Toby's head.

That night, Willow, Freddie and their aunt set up the final window display of the week. It was a Hoozle party scene, with lots of colourful balloons and paper streamers, and the Hoozles themselves, of course, wearing party hats. Toby and Wobbly, Freddie's lion Hoozle, were special guests, and, as Willow went to bed that night, she was sure she could hear the faint sounds of the Hoozles all having a lovely time together,

celebrating and playing in the toy shop window.

It was the perfect ending to a very exciting few days, Willow thought, and she went to sleep with a big smile on her face.

They're not just toys – they're the magical hoozles! And every Hoozle needs a special friend . . .

Collect all these wonderful Hoozle stories!